For my always-on-the-go-family.
And for Jamie—you're awesome!
—L.H.D.

For Jo and Iz!
—R.N.

THIS IS A BORZOI BOOK PUBLISHED BY ALFRED A. KNOPF

Text copyright © 2020 by Lisl H. Detlefsen

Jacket art and interior illustrations copyright © 2020 by Robert Neubecker

All rights reserved. Published in the United States by Alfred A. Knopf, an imprint of Random House Children's Books,
a division of Penguin Random House LLC, New York.

Knopf, Borzoi Books, and the colophon are registered trademarks of Penguin Random House LLC.

Visit us on the Web! rhcbooks.com

Educators and librarians, for a variety of teaching tools, visit us at RHTeachersLibrarians.com

Library of Congress Cataloging-in-Publication Data

Names: Detlefsen, Lisl H., author. | Neubecker, Robert, illustrator.

Title: On the go awesome / by Lisl H. Detlefsen; illustrated by Robert Neubecker.

Description: First edition. | New York: Alfred A. Knopf, 2020. | Summary:
Watching or riding in a variety of vehicles is exciting, but operating each machine is awesome.

Identifiers: LCCN 2019022648 (print) | LCCN 2019022649 (ebook)

ISBN 978-1-9848-5234-2 (hardcover) | ISBN 978-1-9848-5235-9 (library binding) | ISBN 978-1-9848-5236-6 (ebook)

Subjects: CYAC: Vehicles—Fiction.

Classification: LCC PZ7.1.D478 On 2020 (print) | LCC PZ7.1.D478 (ebook) | DDC [E]—dc23

The text of this book is set in 22-point New Baskerville.

The illustrations were created using watercolors, pencils, and a Mac.

Book design by Sarah Hokanson

MANUFACTURED IN CHINA

November 2020   10 9 8 7 6 5 4 3 2 1   First Edition

ON
THE
GO

AWESOME

by **Lisl H. Detlefsen**

illustrated by **Robert Neubecker**

Alfred A. Knopf  New York

Trains are cool.

Watching a train is very cool.

Riding on a train
is even cooler.

But conducting a train through the mountains?

CHUGGA CHUGGA AWESOME!

Excavators are fun.

Watching an excavator is more fun.

Sitting in an excavator is extra fun.

But operating an excavator at a construction site?

Planes are exciting.

Watching planes take off is really exciting.

Flying on a plane is ultra exciting.

But piloting a plane up into the clouds?

Subways are fascinating.

Watching people on the subway platform is fairly fascinating.

Riding the subway is
definitely fascinating.

But operating the subway
far below the bustle
of the big city?

BROADWAY

Monster trucks are major.
Watching monster trucks
is mega major.

Riding in a monster truck
is major to the extreme.

But jumping over a
gigantic row of cars in
a monster truck?

Boats are excellent.

Watching a boat race is more excellent.

Setting sail on a boat is most excellent.

But captaining a boat across the vast ocean?

Rockets are stellar.

Visiting the launchpad to see a rocket is so stellar.

Watching a rocket lift off is super stellar.

But becoming an
astronaut on a rocket?

Campers are cool.
Wait! *Are* campers cool?

Sleeping in a camper is totally cool.
But traveling across the whole
country with your family?

Now, THAT'S awesome.